THIS IGLOO BOOK
BELONGS TO:

Jorsh
....

igloobooks

Published in 2019
by Igloo Books Ltd
Cottage Farm
Sywell
NN6 0BJ
www.igloobooks.com

0819 001.01
2 4 6 8 10 9 7 5 3 1
ISBN 978-1-83852-227-8

Written by Stephanie Moss
Illustrated by Jo Byatt

Designed by Alex Alexandrou
Edited by Hannah Cather

Printed and manufactured in China

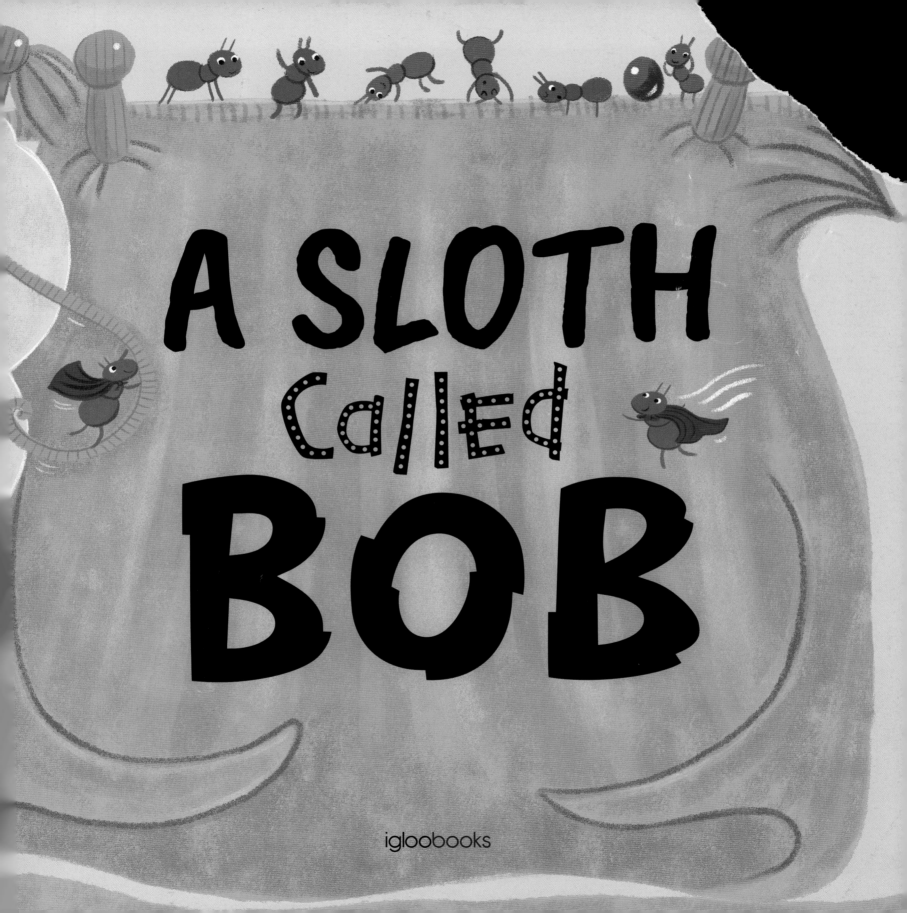

A SLOTH
Called
BOB

igloobooks

Someone

in the dead of night
is putting jungle
wrongs to **right**.

He helps out everywhere he goes.
But **WHO** is he? Nobody knows!

This hero with a secret job...

... is actually... a **SLOTH CALLED BOB!**

His secret isn't
hard to keep.

His friends think
he's always asleep.

"It must be Lion," his friends say, as Bob sneaks off to save the day.

For Lion's **STRONG** and he is **BRAVE**.
Isn't that how heroes behave?

But like all heroes, Bob is kind...

... so he really doesn't mind...

... that no one would ever believe,
the secret he has up his sleeve!

But then one day, Bob is in need
of just one such heroic deed.

His cape goes

RRRRIIIP!

and he gets stuck.

"**Oh, no!**" says Bob.

"**That's just
my luck.**"

As Bob hangs **DANGLING** in the air,
the animals stop to look and stare.

They shout,

THE HERO WILL SAVE YOU!

But Bob **IS** the hero.
What will he do?

So he takes a deep breath,
then counts, **ONE... TWO... THREE...**
"Actually," Bob gulps,
"you're all waiting for... ME!"

Everybody's confused.
This can't be right.

Bob **CAN'T** be the hero who
helps them at night!

Then a breeze shakes the leaves,
till Bob's cape is on view.
The animals all cry,
"It really is you!"

"I may be slow," says Bob. "Yes, that's true.
But sleeping a lot isn't all that I do!"

"When you look past how you saw me before, you'll see what's inside. There's so much more!"

So all of Bob's friends help him down from the tree.
"We know you much better now. Yippee!"

Since then, something strange has occurred.
Everyone's acting differently. Or so we've heard!

The animals feel they can try something new.

Thank you, Super Bob. It's all down to you!

SUPER
BOB